# fuzzbuzz

# More words and letters Level 2

Atlantic Atoll

N
W — E
S

Red Hills

Cliff Top Crags

Mudflats

Stand Still
Inlet

Bad Jack Rockfist

(his map)

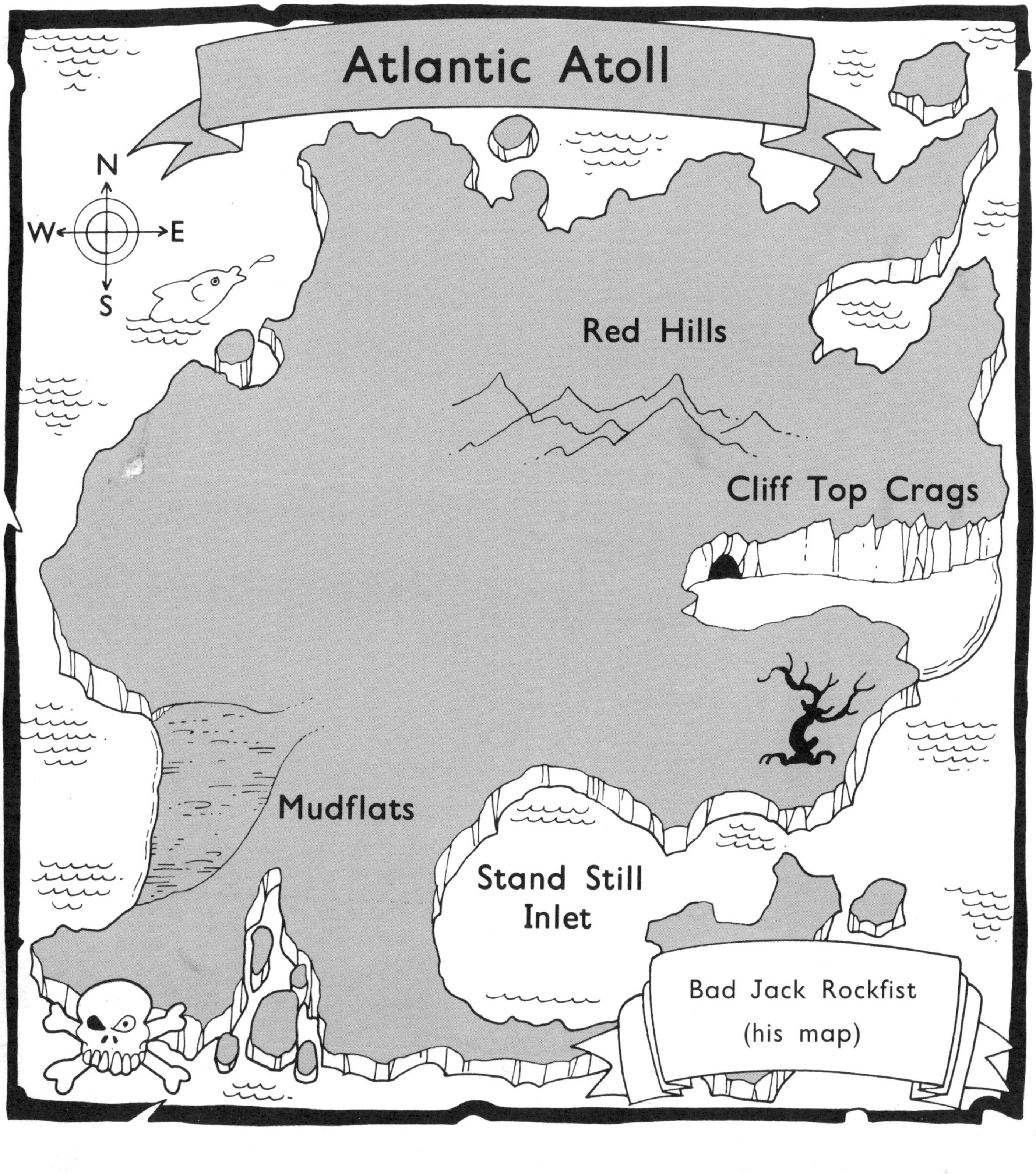

# Teacher's notes

This workbook is designed to be used at the end of Level 2 of the *fuzzbuzz* reading scheme. It follows on from *words 2* and *Letters 2*, but comes before the new work of Level 3 (introduced by *Letters 3*).

It aims to consolidate, revise and develop the work which is covered by the existing Level 2. It does not introduce any new work in terms of either phonics or sight vocabulary: it builds upon the work already learned. But it does assume that the pupils will have completed the core work of Level 2 (storybooks 6 - 12, *letters 1*, *letters 2* and *words 2*).

Unlike the previous workbooks, this book provides a relatively high proportion of continuous reading, ensuring that sight and phonic skills are firmly and inextricably linked to the search for meaning. These passages are followed by questions and instructions which ensure that the pupils must understand, and actually think about, what they are reading throughout.

Because the *fuzzbuzz* children will be able to read every word in this workbook (including all the explanations and instructions) they should be able to use it independently of the teacher: this should be encouraged in order to develop the children's own confidence in themselves.

For the *fuzzbuzz* child this workbook can be used in its own right, as a preparation for the parallel stories of Level 2 (storybooks 12.1 - 12.12), or as a firm foundation for the work of Level 3.

For the non-*fuzzbuzz* child who has already acquired the basic phonic skills, it will provide a valuable link between decoding skills and the over-riding skill of reading for meaning.

More help and advice on how to use this workbook is given in *Using fuzzbuzz*, the teacher's guide to the scheme. It is recommended that every teacher using the scheme should have a copy of this. For a complete list of fuzzbuzz resources please contact OUP Education Dept. at the address below, or telephone 01865 556767.

# More words and letters

Colin Harris

Illustrated by
Mark Farmer

Workbooks and supporting resources in the fuzzbuzz scheme:

**Level 1**
words box 1
Language Master Cards
words 1
100 words

**Level 2**
words box 2
words 2
letters 1
Letters 2
More words and letters
Words for fuzzbuzz facts
Looking at books

**Level 3**
Letters 3
Letters 4
Letters 5

Oxford University Press, Great Clarendon Street, Oxford OX2 6DP

Oxford University Press is a department of the University of Oxford. It furthers the University's objective of excellence in research, scholarship, and education by publishing worldwide in

Oxford New York
Auckland Cape Town Dar es Salaam Hong Kong Karachi Kuala Lumpur Madrid Melbourne Mexico City Nairobi New Delhi Taipei Toronto Shanghai

With offices in
Argentina Austria Brazil Chile Czech Republic France Greece Guatemala Hungary Italy Japan South Korea Poland Portugal Singapore Switzerland Thailand Turkey Ukraine Vietnam

*Oxford* is a registered trade mark of Oxford University Press in the UK and in certain other countries

© Text Colin Harris, Illustrations Mark Farmer 1993

Published 1993
17 16 15

ISBN-13: 978-0-19-838114-3
ISBN-10: 0-19-838114-X

Printed in China

# Contents

# Thrills and spills

This is Samantha Sands. Everyone calls her Sam.
Sam has a very interesting, but very difficult,
job. She does stunts on film sets.

This film is called **The Big Drop** and they are
at the bit of the script where Sam gets shot
and has to drop off the top of a block of flats.
Sam plans everything down to the split second.

At the bottom of the flats, where the camera
cannot see, there is a stack of mattresses for
Sam to land on. And Sam's jacket and pants
have some extra padding. She intends to have a
soft landing!

Hidden in her hand, Sam has a little plastic
bag full of ketchup.

'Get ready!' yells the cameraman. 'Good luck, Sam!'

Up on the top of the block of flats a man acting as
a bad criminal lifts his gun.

CRACK!

Sam clutches her chest and the bag in her hand
splits. Now there is a red blotch on her
jacket and everyone thinks that the bullet has
hit her!

Then Sam goes toppling from the top of the
flats. Down and down she drops, twisting and
spinning.

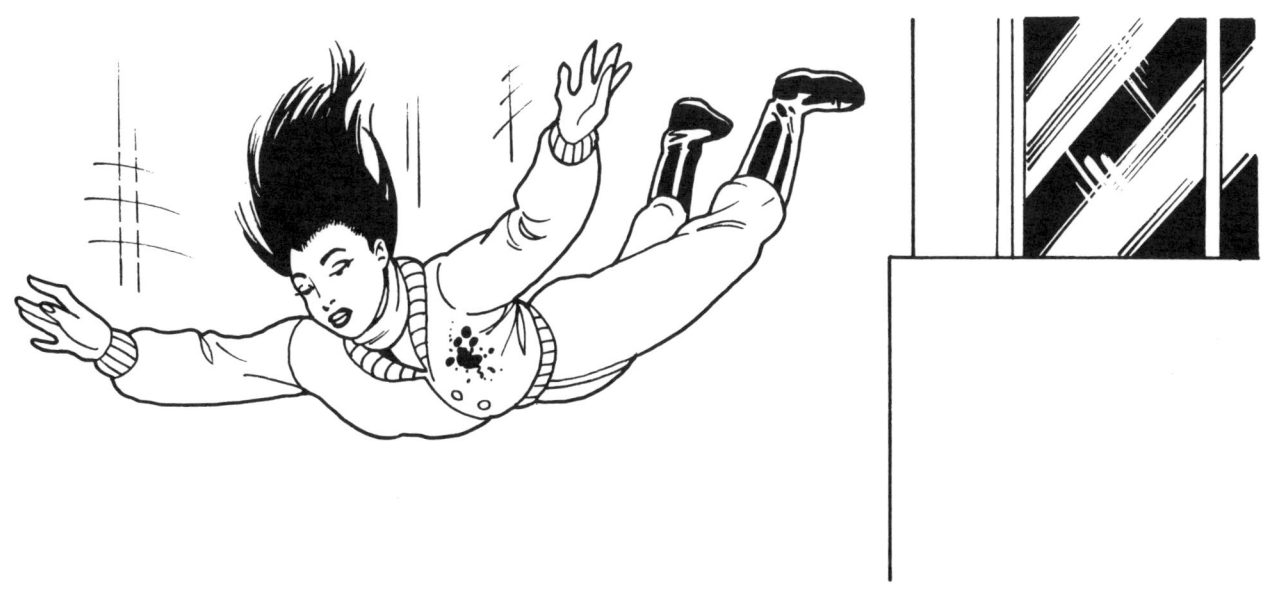

Then, at last, she hits the stack of mattresses
with a soft thwack. As Sam stands up, everyone claps.

'Brilliant!' yells the cameraman. 'But the film got
stuck in the camera. Can you have a second go?'

Can you do these? Do not forget to put capital letters and full stops.

1. What does everyone call Samantha?

_____

2. What is her job?

_____

3. Why do you think that this film is called **The Big Drop**?

_____

4. Why will Sam have a soft landing?

_____

5. What is in the plastic bag?

_____

6. Why does Sam have to have a second go?

_____

7. What do you think a film script is?

_____

8. Have you seen a good film? What is it called?

_____

# Read and draw

Can you draw these?

a parrot cracking a nut

a kestrel dropping onto a rabbit

a blue tit going into a nest box

an ostrich with six big eggs

a thrush with a spotted chest

a pelican catching a fish

7

# Read and draw

Draw these:

two things that will stretch

two things with buttons

two things you can shut

two things you can travel in

two things you can catch

two things you can pump up

two things you can read

two things you can cut with

# In the kitchen

Can you connect the words to the things in the drawing?

jug

sink

mop

shelf

lid

pan

mug

tap

clock

plug

glass

brush

Draw two animals that live in this house.

# Jess and the King

This is Jess.

Colour Jess in.

> His hat is red and blue.
>
> The bells are yellow.
>
> The ruff on his neck is green.
>
> His jacket is red and blue.
>
> The buttons are green.
>
> His pants are red.
>
> His boots are green.

Can you see the bells on Jess's hat?

All Jess has to do is nod, then all the bells ring.

> Ring-a-ding-ding!
>
> Ding-a-ling-a-ling!

Jess has just got a job. It is his first job, and he is in a bit of a flap. He is going to see his boss, and his boss is the King.

This is King Fred. King Fred is not a happy King. In fact, he is a grump. He can have everything he wishes for, but he just sulks.

This is where Jess comes in. His job is to stop the King from sulking. This is a very difficult job.

Jess does tricks, but the King still sulks.

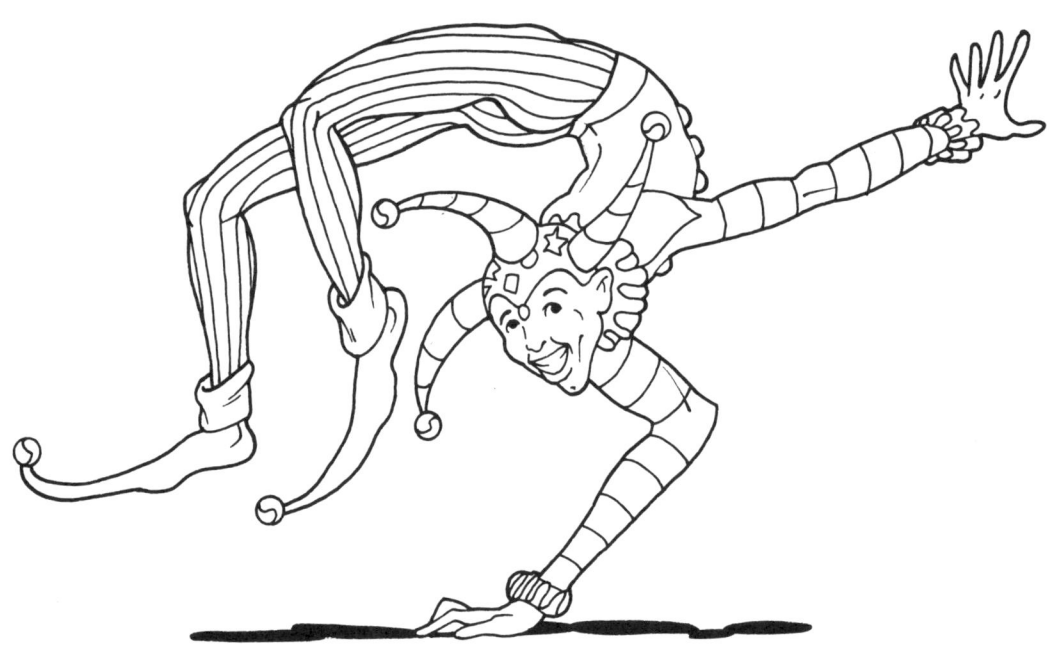

Jess does a handstand, but the King just
huffs and puffs.  So Jess sits and thinks . . . and
thinks . . . and thinks!  And then he thinks of
one last thing!  He goes up to the King and
yells out,

'SIT UP!'

The King blinks and sits up.

'Why do pelicans cost a lot?' yells Jess.

The King blinks, scratches his chin, and thinks.

'Come on,' yells Jess.  'Why do pelicans cost
a lot?'

The King thinks some more.

'Do you give in?' yells Jess.

The King nods.

'Pelicans cost a lot because they have such
big bills!' Jess tells him.

The King blinks, scratches his chin, sucks his bottom lip, and thinks some more.

'What?' asks the King.

'Pelicans cost a lot because they have such big bills!'

And then the King gets it! He claps his hands. He grins. In less than ten seconds he is chuckling.

'That's a good one!' he pants. 'That's a very good one! Ha ha ha!'

At last the King stops.

'That's brilliant! Can you tell some more?'

Jess tells the King that he will tell him some more if the King promises to stop sulking.

'Yes!' nods the King.

So now Jess has got to think of some more!

Can you do these?  Do not forget full stops and capital letters.

1.  What happens if Jess nods?

   _____

2.  What is Jess's boss called?

   _____

3.  What job is Jess expected to do?

   _____

4.  What does Jess do first, and what does the King do?

   _____

   _____

5.  What is the second thing Jess does, and what does the King do?

   _____

   _____

6.  Draw
   a pelican's bill                    a gas bill

# Word sums

| Add two words | Write one word | Draw it |
|---|---|---|
| wind + mill | = <u>windmill</u> | |
| chest + nut | = _____ | |
| rob + in | = _____ | |
| pup + pet | = _____ | |
| fun + gus | = _____ | |
| pump + kin | = _____ | |
| match + box | = _____ | |
| blue + bell | = _____ | |
| hop + scotch | = _____ | |
| ham + mock | = _____ | |

# The vet

If you have a pet animal and it is ill you must go to see the vet. Then the vet will give it a good medical.

If you go to see this vet she will tell you what to do to help the pet. She can inject it, and give it some pills and tablets.

Vets have to read a lot on all the different animal illnesses. They see cats, kittens, dogs, pups, rabbits, parrots, fish, bulls, pigs, hens, ducks, and lots more!

Vets cannot tell what to expect next. This vet has just had to go out to see a dog in a bad traffic smash, and now she is helping a sick duck. And just ready to come and see her is a man with two terrapins in a tank.

She has seen some very odd pets.  One man
called her out to visit an animal that he kept
in the bath!

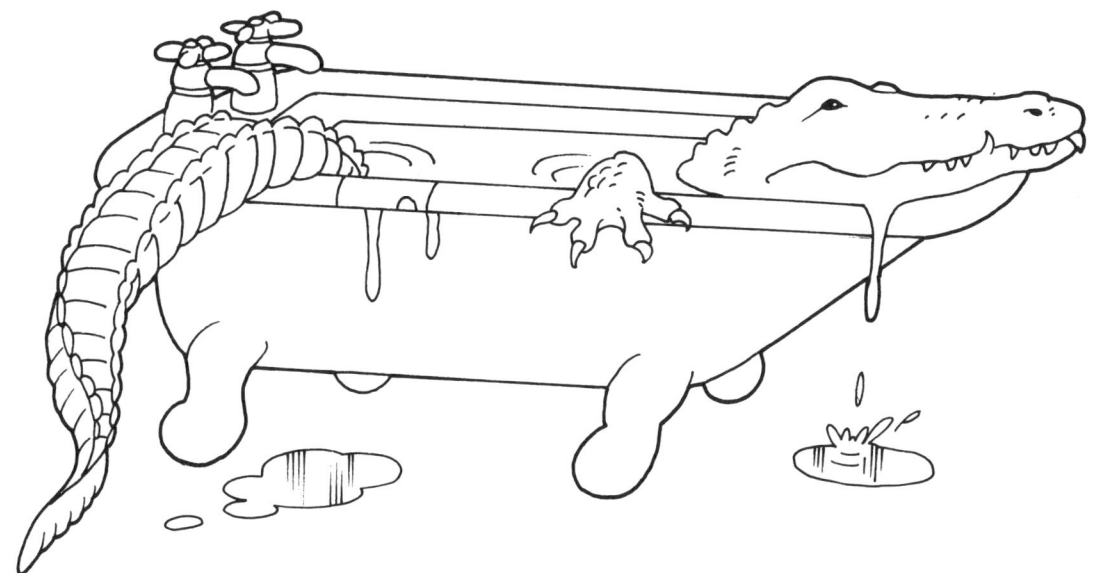

Vets have a very difficult job because animals
cannot tell you if they are ill.

You can tell if an animal is sick if it sleeps
a lot, if it gets very hot and if it does not
eat much.  Then you must go to visit the vet.

1.  Why do vets have a very difficult job?

    _____

2.  What does the man have in the glass tank?

    _____

3.  What tells you that an animal is sick?

    1. _____

    2. _____

    3. _____

# Animals

Can you read these words?

sings        trumpets       buzzes       honks       clucks

snaps        grunts       hisses       yelps

Write the correct word under the animals.

buzzes _____

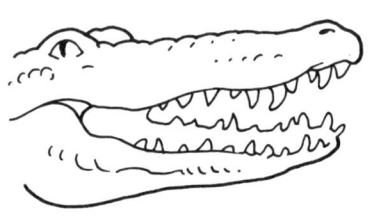

# Idioms

Can you read these sets of words?  They are called idioms.

hopping mad

down in the dumps

costs a packet

coming down in buckets

off colour

doing a bunk

too big for his boots

well off

hit the jackpot

pull his leg

Now see if you can understand them.

Read these and then write in the correct idiom.

1.  If it costs a lot it _____.

2.  If you play a trick on someone you _____.

3.  If someone brags a lot he is _____

    _____.

4.  If you run off you are _____.

5.  If you are ill you are _____.

6.  If you are rich you are _____.

7.  If you are very, very cross you are _____.

8.  If you are sad and glum you are _____

    _____.

9.  If you win a lot of cash you _____.

10.  If it is so wet it is pelting down, it is _____

    _____.

# The one-man-band

Tom Smith had a good job as an assistant in a big model shop, selling model kits to happy children.

Then things got bad and the shop had to shut. Tom lost his job.  He went everywhere hunting for a job but lots more shops had shut and all the jobs had run out.

Now Tom is very sad.  He sits down and does a lot of thinking.  If he cannot get a job, he must think of a job for himself.

Tom is good at playing instruments, so he thinks he will have a go at busking.  Busking is standing next to a big shop and playing for everyone going past.

So Tom goes up into his attic to hunt for his
instruments. There is dust everywhere, but
Tom can still see the things he must get.

Tom gives everything a good polish.
Now Tom must think of dressing himself up.
He must stand out so that everyone can see him.
So he collects some stuff and puts it on his bed.

Tom gets ready. He puts everything into a big chest, and sets off for the shops.

Now Tom gets into his outfit. He attaches some of the instruments to himself and picks up the rest.

Everyone loves him. They stop for a bit, and then they drop some cash into his hat. In the end, the hat is full to the top. Tom is happy at last!

1. What did Tom do for his first job?

   _____

2. Tom lost his job.   Why?

   _____

   _____

3. What is busking?

   _____

   _____

4. Write down six things in Tom's attic.

   _____        _____

   _____        _____

   _____        _____

5. Write down six things Tom put on his bed.

   _____        _____

   _____        _____

   _____        _____

6. What is dangling from:

   1.  Tom's vest        _ _ _ - _ _ _ _

   2.  Tom's belt        _ _ l l _

   3.  Tom's drumstick        _ _ p p _ _

# Hats

Tom had two hats to dress up in.  These are some more hats.  Can you read the words at the bottom and then write under the hats what they are called?

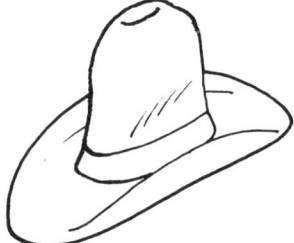

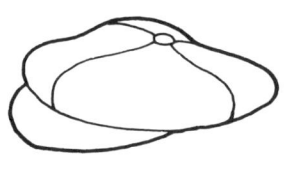

_____

_____

_____

_____

_____

_____

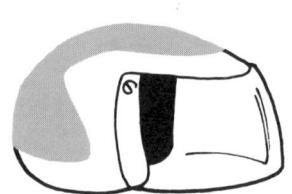

_____

_____

_____

| bonnet | fez | ten-gallon hat |
|--------|-----|----------------|
| helmet | pom-pom hat | Santa's hat |
| top hat | flat cap | witch's hat |

# Problem solving

Read these words, then have a go at solving the
problems at the bottom.

cot        tent      loft          fish       kiln      glasses

milk       clock     cannibals     lift       bin       humps

gift       egg       lipstick      matches    skunk     bulb

1.  It goes up and down.            It is a _____.
2.  A word for present.             _____.
3.  You put rubbish in it.          _____.
4.  You put it in a lamp.           _____.
5.  It has two hands.               _____.
6.  It is at the top of the house.  _____.
7.  You drink it.                   _____.
8.  Little ones sleep in it.        _____.
9.  You get hot pots out of it.     _____.
10. A chick comes out of it.        _____.
11. You can camp in it.             _____.
12. It goes well with chips.        _____.
13. This animal smells bad.         _____.
14. It is for colouring lips.       _____.

15. They help you to see.           They are _____.
16. Some camels have two.           _____.
17. They eat you.                   _____.
18. Do not play with these.         _____.

# The hippopotamus

This animal is a hippopotamus.  That is a very big word for a very big animal!  The hippopotamus has little, fat legs and very thick, greenish-black skin.

The hippopotamus lives in African rivers.
It eats green plants, and it loves grass the best of all.  It pulls the grass up with its thick lips.

If the hippopotamus gets too hot, it stretches out on the thick brown mud next to the river bank and has a little nap.

The hippopotamus does not just swim in the river.  It can sink down to the bottom, so that it is standing on the river bed.

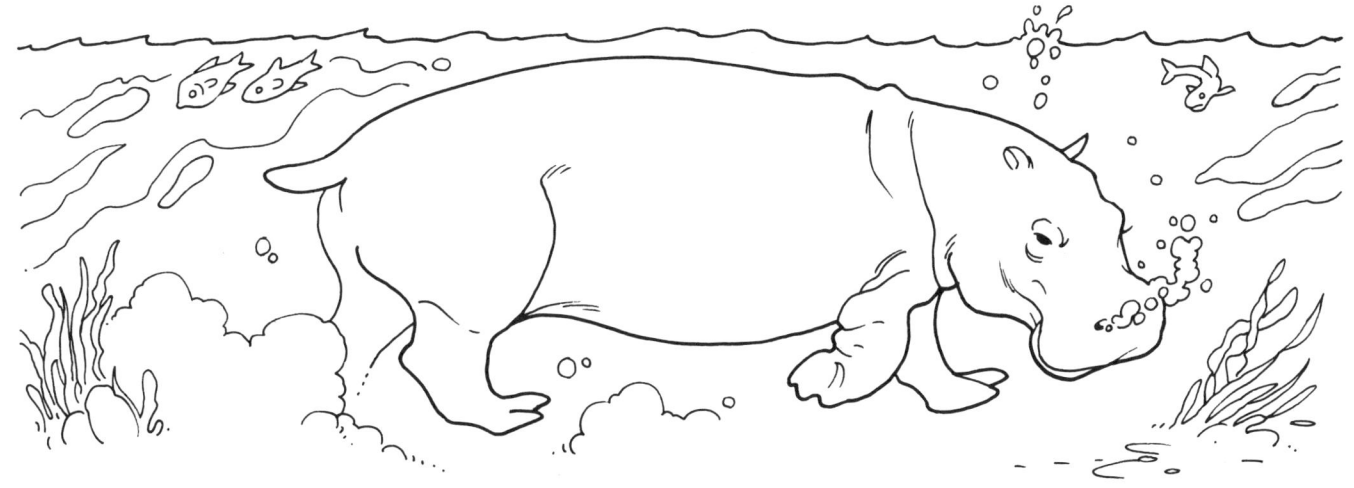

It is astonishing, but the hippopotamus can trot across the river bed just as well as it can trot on the land.

1.  Where does the hippopotamus live?

    _____

2.  What colour is it?

    _____

3.  What does it love to eat best?

    _____

4.  What does it do if it gets too hot?

    _____

    _____

5.  How does it travel across rivers?

    _____

    _____

# Doing words

Can you spot what all these children are doing?
Write the 'doing words' on the dashes under the
drawings.

_ _ n n _ _ _ _      _ _ p p _ _ _      _ _ _ p p _ _ _

_ _ _ _ _ _ _      _ _ _ _ _ _ _      _ _ _ p p _ _ _

_ _ t t _ _ _      _ _ _ _ _ _ _      _ _ _ _ _ _ _

28

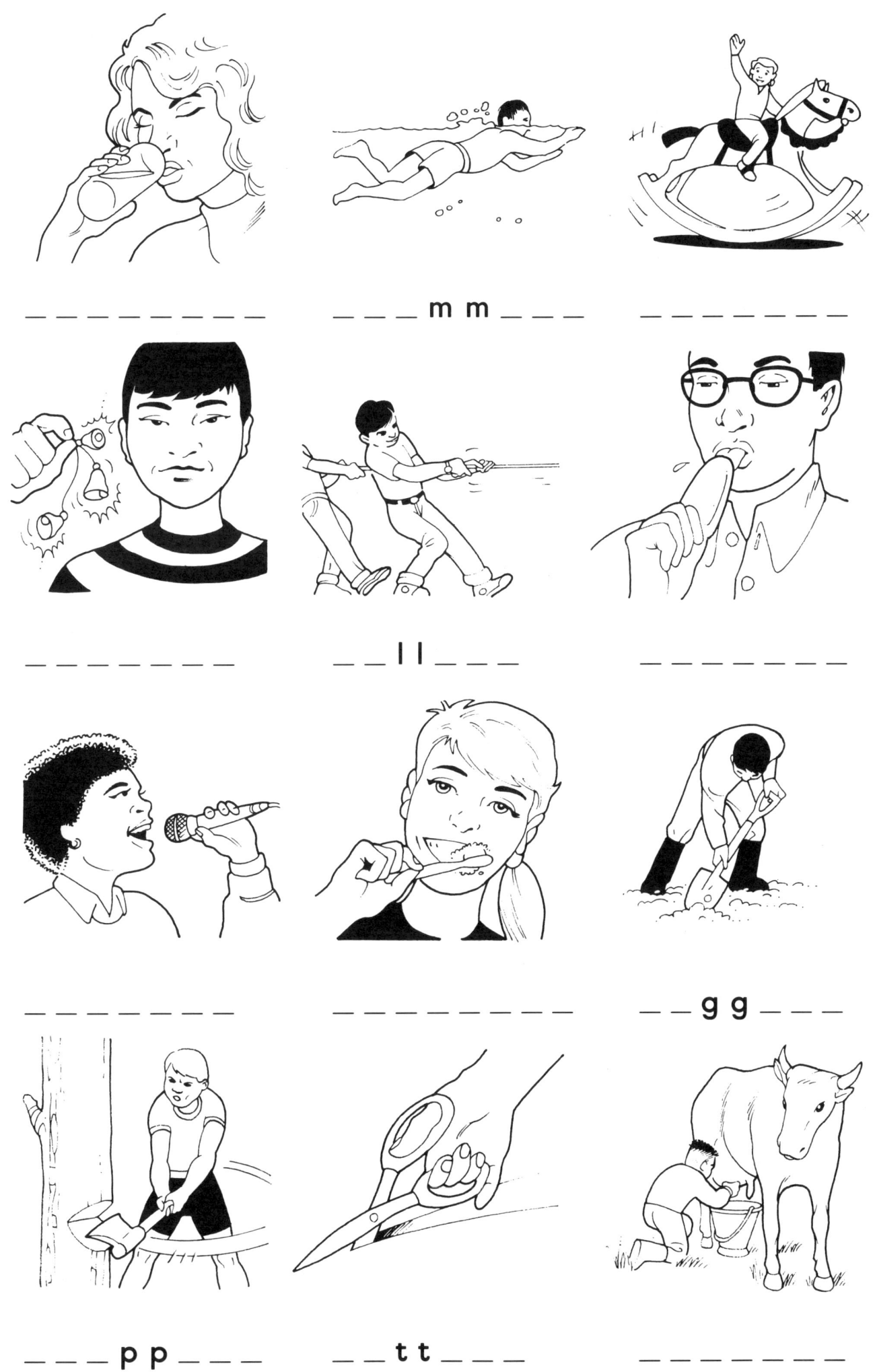

_ _ _ _ _ _ _     _ _ m m _ _ _     _ _ _ _ _ _

_ _ _ _ _ _ _     _ _ l l _ _ _     _ _ _ _ _ _ _

_ _ _ _ _ _ _     _ _ _ _ _ _ _     _ _ g g _ _ _

_ _ _ p p _ _ _     _ _ t t _ _ _     _ _ _ _ _ _ _

# The lollipop man

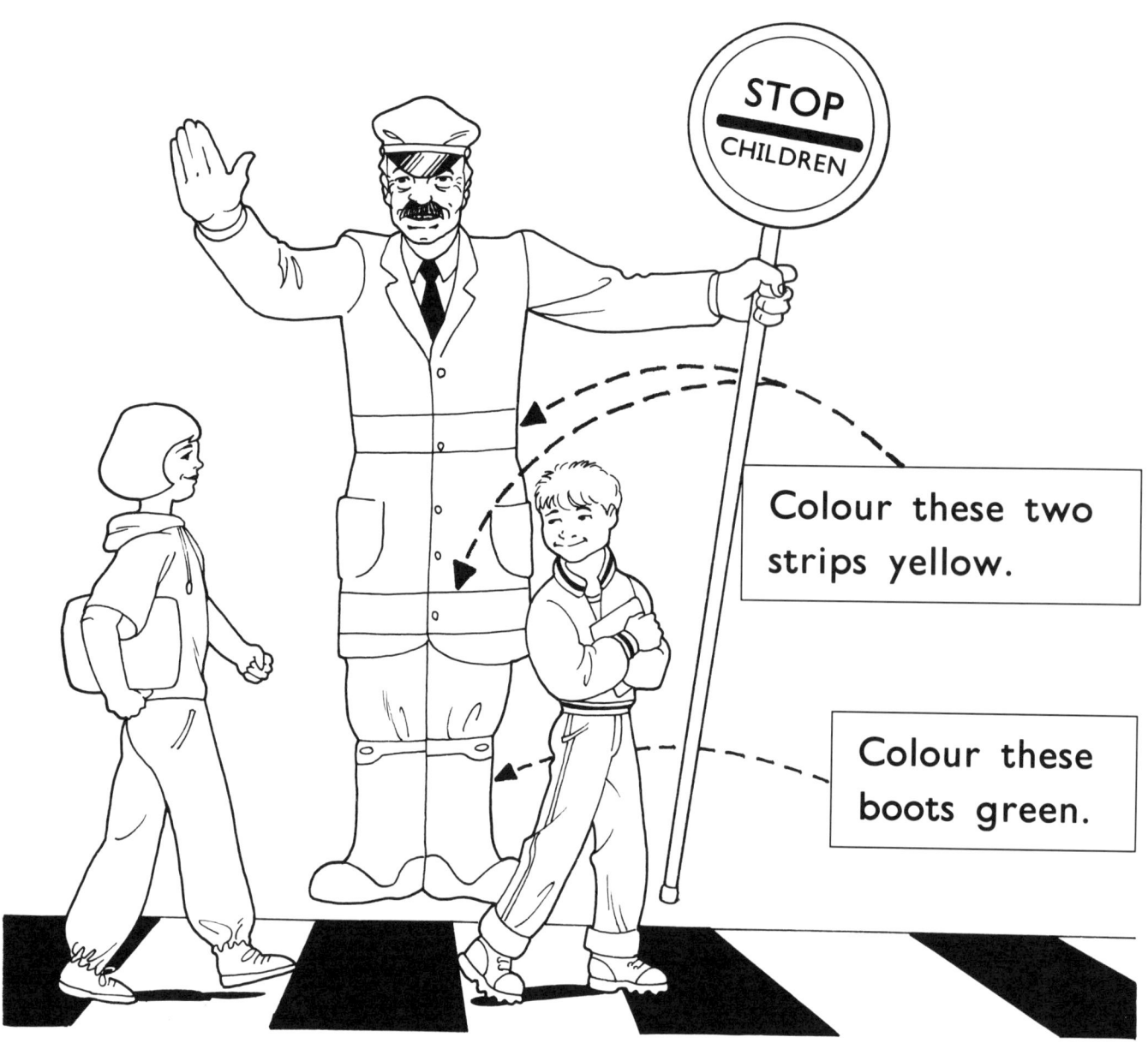

Colour these two strips yellow.

Colour these boots green.

This man is called Ted Brown but all the children call him the lollipop man.

He has big green boots, a plastic mac and a cap.  There are yellow strips on his mac so that the traffic can see him.

Ted helps the children to go across the zebra crossing.

He stands on the crossing and lifts up his stick.
The traffic stops to let the children go across.

The children think that Ted's stick is a
big lollipop.  That is why he is called the
lollipop man.

Can you read the words at the top of his stick?

Can you do these?  Do not forget capital
letters and full stops.

1.  What is this man called?

_____

2.  What do the children call him?

_____

3.  Why does Ted have yellow strips on his mac?

_____

4.  Draw the top of Ted's stick and write the words on it.

# What goes into them?

Can you read these words?

parrot      bulb      hand      rabbit      egg

rubbish      fish      petrol      picnic      milk

shopping      plant      jam      hot drink

Now do this.

The boxes are in sets of two. In one box is
an object. In the next box you must draw
something from the list at the top that goes
into that object. Then write the correct word
under the box.

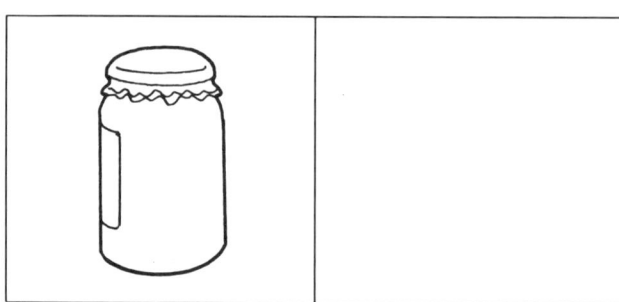

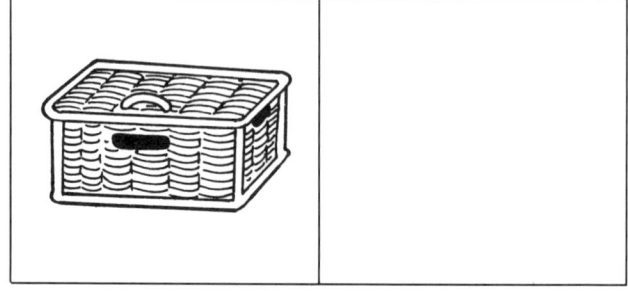

# You

What are you called? _____

Where do you live? _____

_____

_____

_____

_____

In box 1, draw you, in the things you have on now.

In box 2, draw where you live.  Draw this as
well as you can.

In box 3, draw where you sleep.  Draw all the
things that are next to the bed.

In box 4, draw a helpful job that you do in the house.

In box 5, draw something that you love to eat.

In box 6, draw the last present you got.

In box 7, draw something that you play with.

In box 8, draw someone that you play with.

In box 9, draw something that you love to put on.

In box 10, draw you in the lesson you love best.

1.

2.

3.

4.

5.

6.

7.

8.

9.

10.

# The pickpocket

The little man is a pickpocket. The big man standing next to him helps him.

The pickpocket creeps up to you in shops and at bus stops. He pretends to bump into you and in less than ten seconds he lifts all the cash you have on you.

His hands are very fast, so you cannot tell what he is doing. He does not put the things he gets into his pocket. He passes them on to the big man as fast as he can. This is very cunning. If someone catches him he will have nothing on him and they will have to let him go.

The big man slips all the stuff into his bag, and they go back to the house. They get out the things they have collected.

They put all the cash into a cash-box, and they will sell the rest of the stuff.

1. What does the little man do?

   _____

2. How does the big man help him?

   _____

3. Where do the men put the cash?

   _____

4. Draw the little man picking someone's pocket.

# More word sums

| Add two words | Write one word | Draw it |
|---|---|---|
| lip + stick | = <u>lipstick</u> | |
| tab + lets | = _____ | |
| mam + moth | = _____ | |
| mat + tress | = _____ | |
| hum + bugs | = _____ | |
| green + house | = _____ | |
| letter + box | = _____ | |
| drum + stick | = _____ | |
| hand + cuffs | = _____ | |
| trip + lets | = _____ | |

# The frogman

Can you connect the words to the things in the drawing?

mask

tank

belt

net

crab

flatfish

sand

rock

shell

1. The frogman's belt is full of metal.  Why do you think this is?

_____

_____

2. What does he have on his back?

_____

_____

3. What do you think he is going to catch?

_____

_____

# Odd-one-out

Read these lists of words. In every list, one word does not fit. Can you spot the odd-one-out? If you can, cross it out.

1. hat socks jacket vest mittens dishcloth

2. apple melon plum sandwich lemon

3. rabbit thrush robin gull kestrel heron

4. red green pink blue flag yellow

5. Tom Carol Bill Alan Kevin Adam

6. box sack bag carrots can packet

7. leg hip hand bottom neck desk

8. Holland Atlantic America Scotland India

9. flatfish haddock cod halibut frog

10. pram ticket minibus taxi truck van

11. clogs mittens sandals flip-flops boots

12. caramel gumdrop lollipop mint ham

13. cricket golf trunks tennis badminton

14. Smith Atkins Hobbs Emma Pitt

15. cup glass mug jug bluebell

# Read and draw

Can you draw these things?

a gull attacking a crab

some mugs on a rack

a criminal in prison

some fragments of glass

a dog fetching a stick

someone doing the splits

# Bringing the milk

This is Belinda Dixon. Belinda gets out of bed as the sun comes up. She goes out in fog, wet and wind, to bring fresh milk to everyone's step.

First of all, she has to stack the milk on her electric milk van. Then she can set off. Her van does not have to go very fast because she has to stop a lot.

Belinda sells some extra things such as pop, eggs, orange drinks and chickens in plastic bags.

It is not a good thing to let the milk sit on the step. If the sun is hot, the milk can go off, and then it is very bad to drink.

If the blue tits spot it they will peck into the metal top and have a drink.  Blue tits love milk!

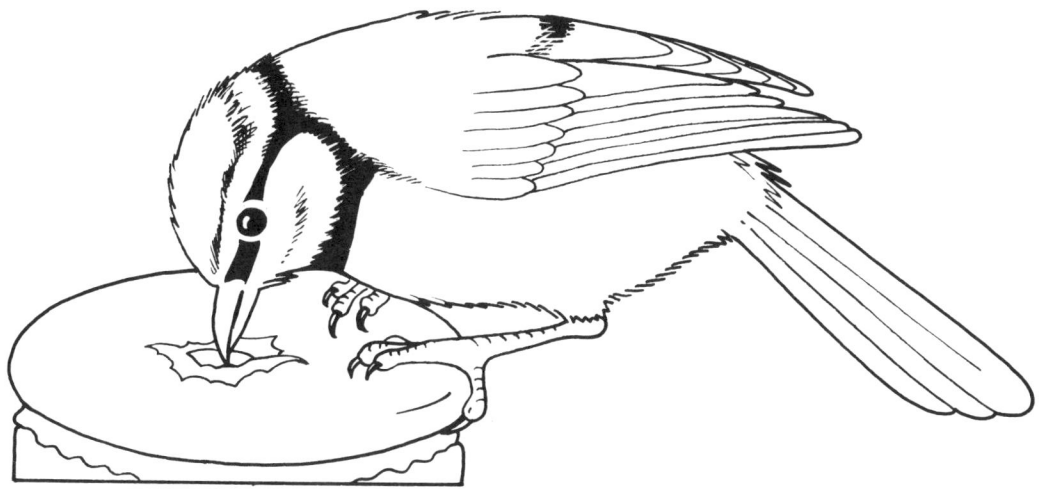

1.  What job does Belinda do?

   _____

2.  Does her van run on petrol?

   _____

3.  What happens to milk if it is left out in the hot sun?

   _____

4.  How do blue tits get at the milk?

   _____

5.  Draw 3 extra things that Belinda sells.

| | | |
|---|---|---|
| | | |

# Big and little letters

Can you read these?

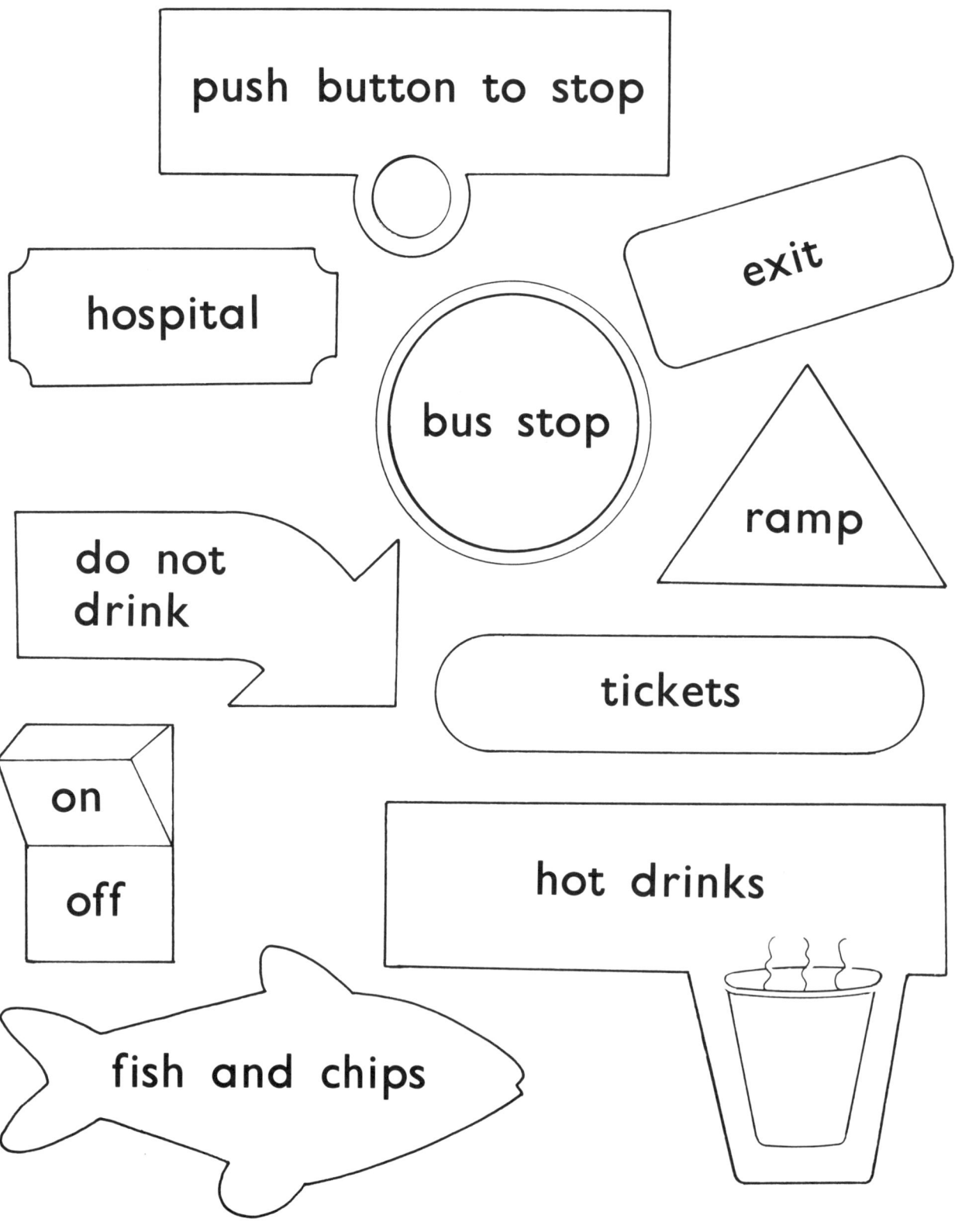

push button to stop

hospital

exit

bus stop

ramp

do not
drink

tickets

on

off

hot drinks

fish and chips

Now write all the words out in capital letters.

# Gran's garden

Grandma Ramsbottom lives in a little red-brick house called **The Elms**. It has two big elm trees standing next to it. The house is little, but the garden is very big. Grandma loves gardening.

She has a rock garden, several patches of grass, six plastic tubs and lots of shrubs and trees. There is a plot of land at the back where she can plant some fresh greens.

Grandma has a shed for her plant pots, compost and baskets. She has a greenhouse too.

Grandma has two grandchildren called Beth and Justin.  They often come to visit her.  Justin helps Grandma with the planting, but Beth just loves to get up into the trees and help herself to apples and plums.

Can you do these?  Do not forget full stops and capital letters.

1.  What is Grandma's house called?

_____

2.  Why do you think it is called this?

_____

3.  What colour is the house?

_____

4.  What does Grandma love to do?

_____

5.  What is in her shed?

_____

_____

6.  What are her grandchildren called?

_____

# Ticks and crosses

Read these.  Some are correct and some are not.
If you think that they are correct, put a tick in the box.
If they are incorrect, put a cross.

☑ ? ☒

| | |
|---|---|
| 1. | Ducks can swim. | ☐ |
| 2. | Some camels have two humps. | ☐ |
| 3. | Frost is hot. | ☐ |
| 4. | Apples have pips. | ☐ |
| 5. | Grass is blue. | ☐ |
| 6. | Skunks stink. | ☐ |
| 7. | Carrots are orange. | ☐ |
| 8. | Some children play hopscotch. | ☐ |
| 9. | All adults are children at first. | ☐ |
| 10. | One and one is two. | ☐ |
| 11. | Two and two is six. | ☐ |
| 12. | All jackets have buttons. | ☐ |
| 13. | Mammoths are extinct now. | ☐ |
| 14. | Zebras are spotted. | ☐ |
| 15. | Spotted dogs are spotted. | ☐ |
| 16. | Javelins are animals that run very fast. | ☐ |
| 17. | Rockets land on plants. | ☐ |
| 18. | Little cats are called mittens. | ☐ |

# Bits of us

Can you read the words under all these boxes?
Now draw the different bits of us in the correct boxes.

We see with these.

We smell with this.

We eat with these.

We kick with these.

We put a hat on this.

We can scratch with these.

We pick things up
with these.

We have to get this cut
every so often.

# Bad Jack Rockfist

This is Bad Jack Rockfist.   He is standing on the deck of his ship.   Bad Jack Rockfist is a very wicked man.   He has pistols in his belt and a cutlass in his hand.

Can you see something hidden in his boot?   Bad Jack lost the bottom of his left leg battling with an octopus.   Now he has a peg leg.

He has a black patch and a black hat. Can you see the skull on his hat?

Bad Jack's ship is called **The Gull**.

Write the words **The Gull** in the box you can
see on the hull.

Colour the hull and the masts brown.

Colour the bell yellow.

Colour the cannon black.

Draw Bad Jack standing next to the cannon.

Bad Jack rests in his hammock so he can see his men scrubbing the decks and polishing the brass. He insists that everyone must do a good job.

The men stand trembling as Bad Jack checks everything. If someone has left a mess, Bad Jack punishes him.

'Bring out the plank!' yells Bad Jack.

He pushes the man onto the plank and prods him with the cutlass.

Then     SPLASH!

The man goes under.

Every man does his best to do a good job on Bad Jack's ship!

Bad Jack loves to attack Spanish galleons.

Shots from his cannon smash the mast and the galleon must stop.  Bad Jack and his men jump onto the galleon and rob it.  Then they sink it!

Down in his cabin Bad Jack has a chest full of Spanish riches.  In it there are goblets, crosses, lockets, pendants and nuggets.

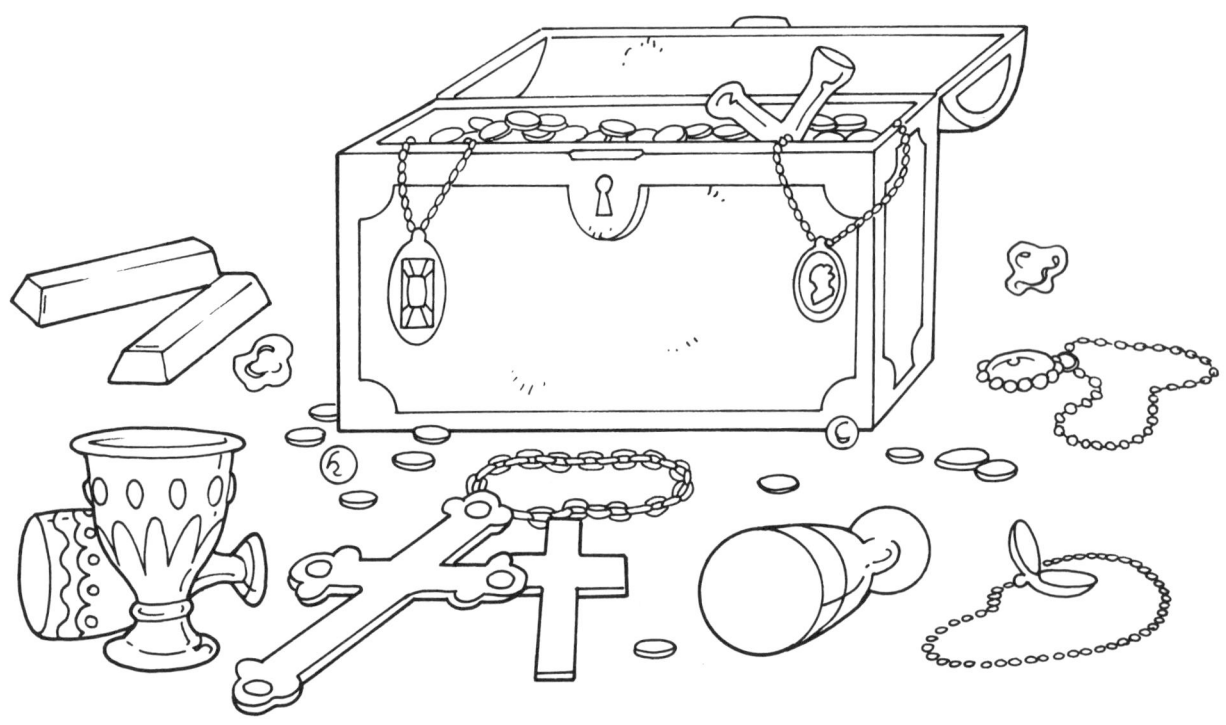

Now and then, a galleon sinks too fast, and Bad Jack cannot rob it.  So he draws a map of the exact spot where the ship sank, and at the bottom he writes:

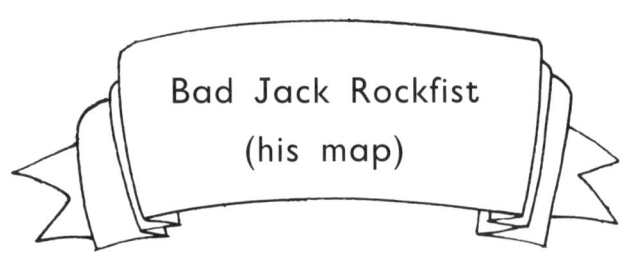

Bad Jack Rockfist
(his map)

So if you come across a map with these words on the bottom, and it tells you where a sunken galleon is, you will end up very, very rich.
Good hunting!

Can you do these?   Do not forget full stops and capital letters.

1.  What does Bad Jack have hidden in his boot?

_____

2.  Why does he have a peg leg?

_____

3.  What is Bad Jack's ship called?

_____

4.  What does Bad Jack do to punish his men?

_____

_____

5.  What does he do if a ship sinks too fast?

_____

_____

6.  Draw a locket, a pendant and a nugget.

|  |  |  |
|---|---|---|
|  |  |  |

# Read and draw

It has six legs.

It has two wings.

It is yellow and black.

It stings.

You get everything off.

You stand in it.

You switch it on.

You get very wet.

It runs downhill.

It is wet.

It has a bed.

Fish live in it.

You get a pen.

You write an address on it.

You stick a stamp on it.

You send it off.

It is green.

You cut it in summer.

You can play cricket on it.

You go there a lot.

You have to sit down.

There are lessons to do.

# Some more word sums

| Add two words | Write one word | Draw it |
|---|---|---|
| gob + let | = goblet | |
| sun + set | = _____ | |
| can + non | = _____ | |
| chop + sticks | = _____ | |
| had + dock | = _____ | |
| ketch + up | = _____ | |
| hand + bag | = _____ | |
| but + ton | = _____ | |
| dust + pan | = _____ | |
| grand + stand | = _____ | |

# The athletics match

There are lots of things happening in this athletics match. Can you spot them all?
Now read these. Some of them are correct and some are not. Put a tick in the box if it is correct, and a cross if it is incorrect.

✓ ? ✗

1. The men on the running track are passing on a bag of humbugs. ☐

2. They are passing on a baton. ☐

3. The British men will win. ☐

4. The American men will win. ☐

5. The man with the javelin has a black vest. ☐

6. The man with the discus has a black vest. ☐

7. The sand pit is for playing in. ☐

8. The sand pit is to give a soft landing. ☐

9. The man with the black hat has a sandwich in his hand. ☐

10. The man with the black hat has a gun in his hand. ☐

11. Jill is standing still. ☐

12. Jill is running off. ☐

What is going to happen to Jill?

# Bad Jack's chest

The chest in Bad Jack's cabin is full up, and
Bad Jack hunts for somewhere to put all the
riches until he can come back for them. Then
he draws a map so that he will not forget where
the chest is hidden.

This is the map.

Bad Jack has left a lot of things out of the map.
Can you finish it off?

1.  At the top of the Atoll, past the Red Hills,
    there is a thick forest.  Draw it and write
    **The Forbidden Forest** next to it.

2.  A river, with lots of bends, runs from the Red
    Hills to the Mudflats on the west of the Atoll.
    Draw it and write **Red River** next to it.

3.  At one end of the Atoll is an inlet called
    Stand Still Inlet.  This is where Bad Jack
    docks his ship.  Draw his ship resting there.

4.  A path goes from Stand Still Inlet past a black
    and twisted tree to Cliff Top Crags.  Draw it.

5.  At the bottom of the cliffs is a tunnel.  Write
    **Black Bat Tunnel** next to it.  There are some
    skulls and a skeleton at the bottom of the
    cliff too.  Draw them.

6.  Last of all, Bad Jack has forgotten to draw
    the spot where he hid the chest.  Draw a red
    cross where you think the chest is hidden.

# Pets

Can you draw these pets?

a pet that lives in a
hutch

a pet that sleeps in a
kennel

a pet that drinks milk

a pet with a shell that
lives in the garden

a pet that chirrups and
sings

a pet that lives in a glass
tank

# Spot what's missing

Can you see what is missing from these drawings? The words at the bottom will help you. Write the correct words under the drawings, then draw the missing bits.

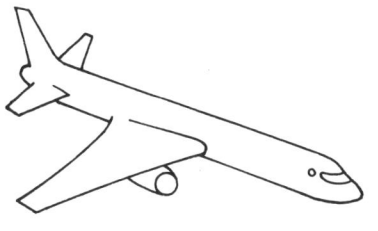

_____

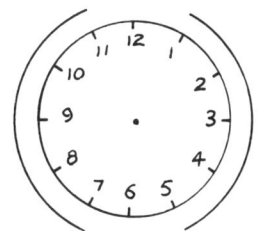

_____

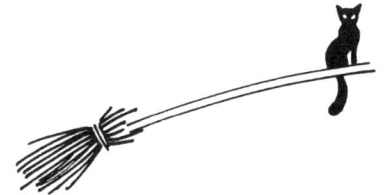

_____

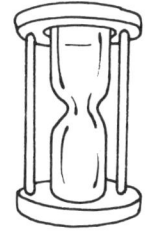

_____

_____

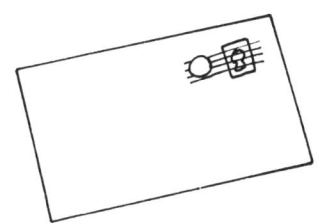

_____

_____

_____

_____

_____

_____

_____

| words | address | helmet | wing | chessmen | button |
| witch | fish | hands | sand | children | leg |

# A pocketful of things

What are these?   Can you write the words?

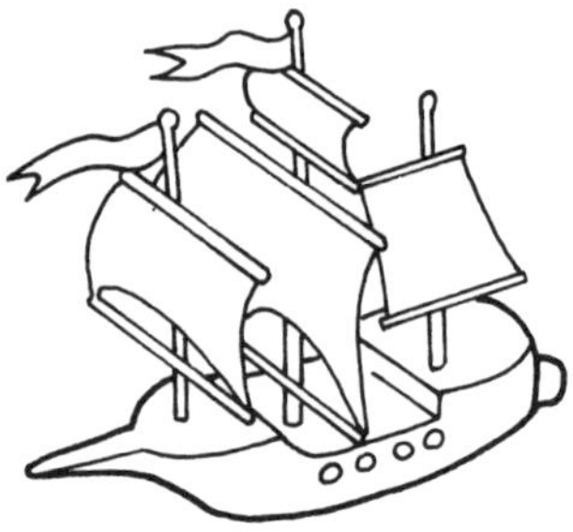

_ _ _ _ _

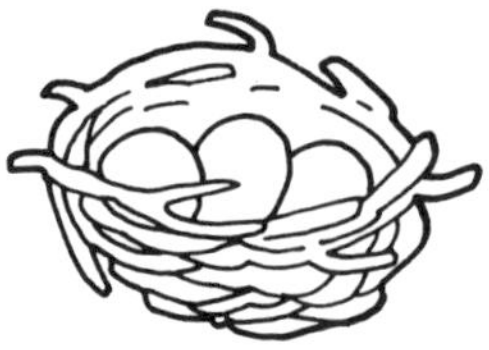

_ _ _ _ _

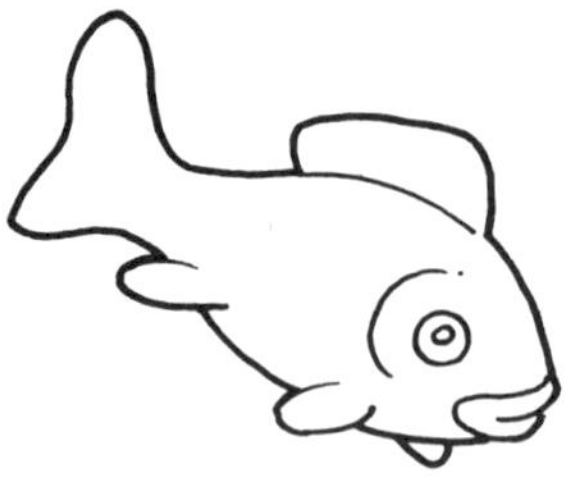

_ _ _ _ _

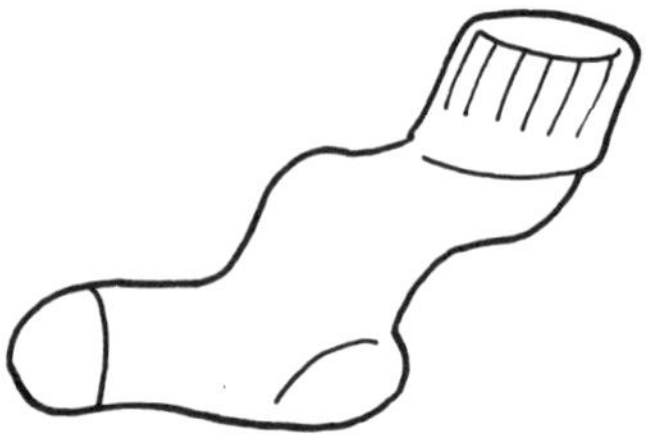

_ _ _ _ _

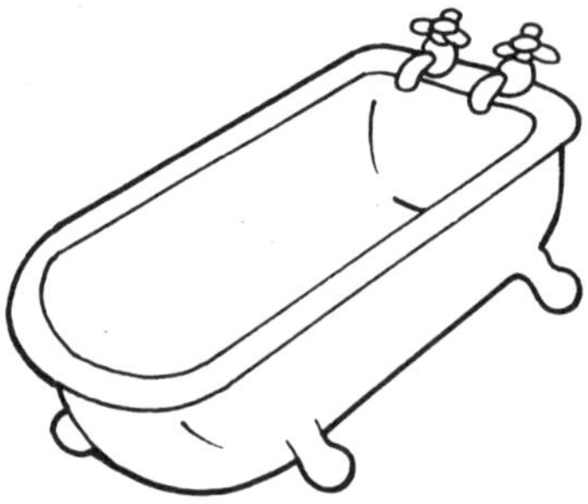

_ _ _ _ _

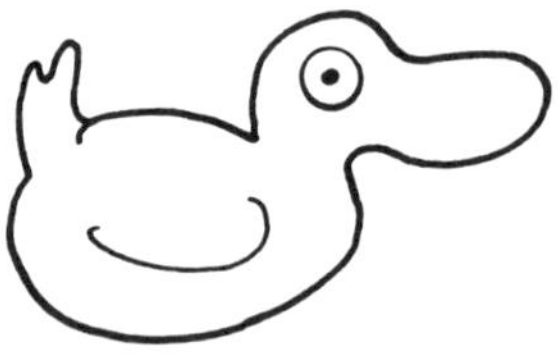

_ _ _ _ _

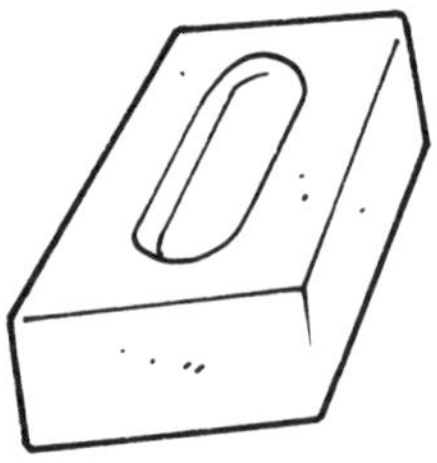

_ _ _ _ _

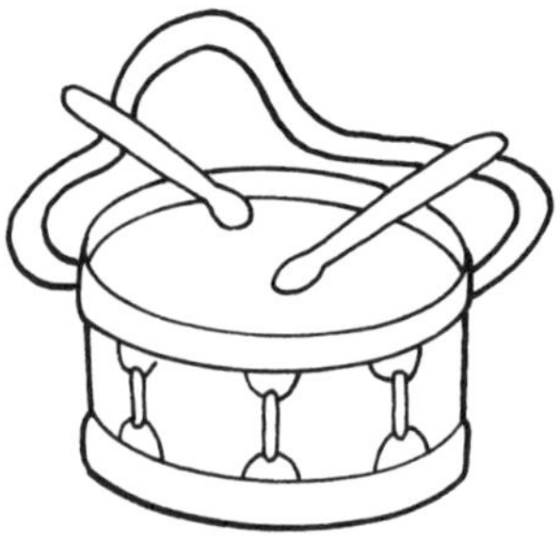

_ _ _ _ _

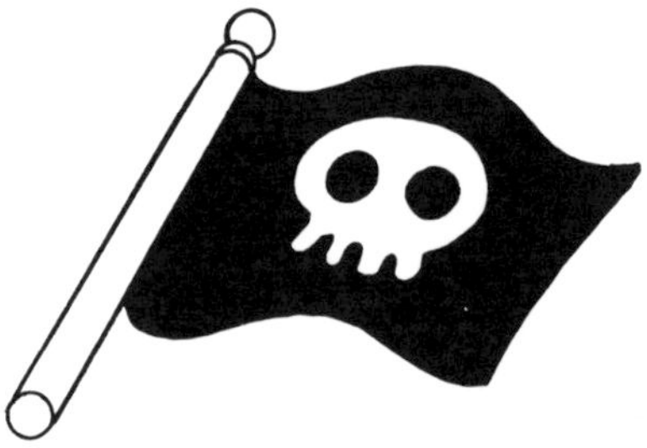

_ _ _ _ _

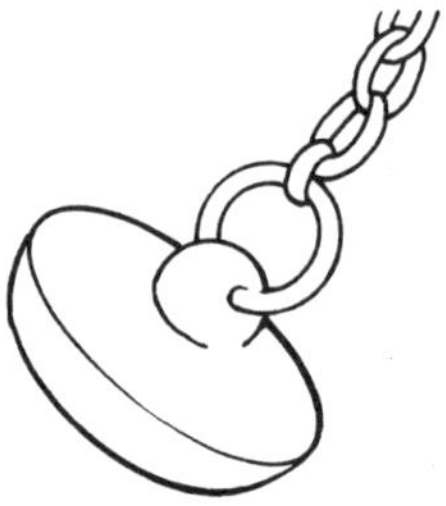

_ _ _ _ _

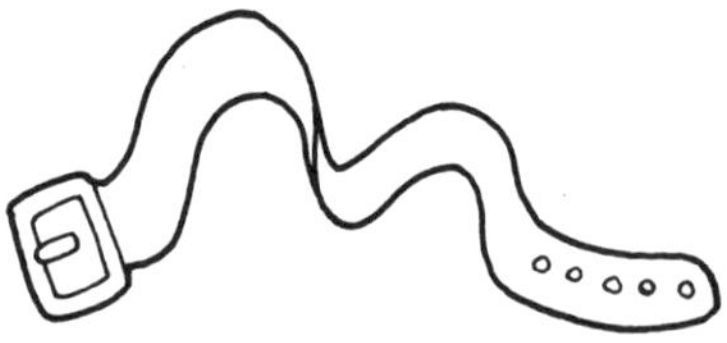

_ _ _ _ _

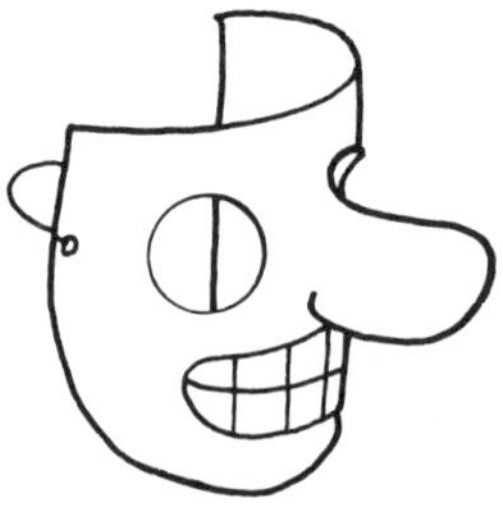

_ _ _ _ _

Can you tell where they have
all come from?

64

ISBN 0-19-838114-X

9 780198 381143